To Jon Scieszka
(who also can't dance)

First Edition, June 2009
20 19 18 17 16 15 14 13 12 11
FAC-029191-16015

Library of Congress Cataloging-in-Publication Data on file.
ISBN 978-1-4231-1410-9

Visit www.hyperionbooksforchildren.com and www.pigeonpresents.com

Elephants Cannot Dance!

An **ELEPHANT & PIGGIE** Book

By **Mo Willems**

Hyperion Books for Children/*New York*
AN IMPRINT OF DISNEY BOOK GROUP

Let's dance!

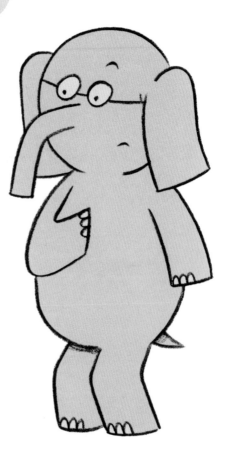

4

9

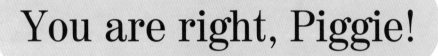

You are right, Piggie!

I *can* try to dance!

zip!

18

19

Okay. Let's go.

Jump with me when
I count to three.

25

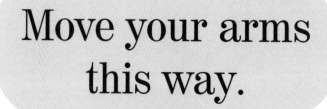

Move your arms
this way.

Lift your leg
this way.

35

37

41

Oh, Gerald . . .

Hello-o-o-o-o-o!

We are ready to learn some moves!

I am sorry. I cannot teach you now.

My friend is sad.

Silly! We do not want *you* to teach us!

We want to learn "The Elephant"!

Teach me, please!

Me too!

Elephant and Piggie have more funny adventures in: